margaret Tempest.

GREY RABBIT AND THE
WANDERING HEDGEHOG

Little Grey Rabbit Books

SQUIRREL GOES SKATING
WISE OWL'S STORY
LITTLE GREY RABBIT'S PARTY
THE KNOT SQUIRREL TIED
FUZZYPEG GOES TO SCHOOL
LITTLE GREY RABBIT'S CHRISTMAS
MOLDY WARP THE MOLE
HARE JOINS THE HOME GUARD
LITTLE GREY RABBIT'S WASHING DAY
WATER RAT'S PICNIC
LITTLE GREY RABBIT'S BIRTHDAY
THE SPECKLEDY HEN
LITTLE GREY RABBIT TO THE RESCUE (*Play*)
LITTLE GREY RABBIT AND THE WEASELS
GREY RABBIT AND THE WANDERING HEDGEHOG
LITTLE GREY RABBIT MAKES LACE
HARE AND THE EASTER EGGS
LITTLE GREY RABBIT'S VALENTINE
LITTLE GREY RABBIT GOES TO THE SEA
HARE AND GUY FAWKES
LITTLE GREY RABBIT'S PAINT BOX
GREY RABBIT FINDS A SHOE
GREY RABBIT AND THE CIRCUS
GREY RABBIT'S MAY DAY
HARE GOES SHOPPING
LITTLE GREY RABBIT'S PANCAKE DAY

Illustrated by Katherine Wigglesworth
LITTLE GREY RABBIT GOES TO THE NORTH POLE
FUZZYPEG'S BROTHER
LITTLE GREY RABBIT'S SPRING CLEANING PARTY
LITTLE GREY RABBIT AND THE SNOW BABY

Grey Rabbit & the Wandering Hedgehog

by Alison Uttley
Pictures by Margaret Tempest

Collins London

FIRST PUBLISHED 1948
THIRTEENTH IMPRESSION 1982

ISBN 0 00 194115 1

COPYRIGHT RESERVED
PRINTED IN GREAT BRITAIN
WILLIAM COLLINS SONS & CO LTD GLASGOW

FOREWORD

OF course you must understand that Grey Rabbit's home had no electric light or gas, and even the candles were made from pith of rushes dipped in wax from the wild bees' nests, which Squirrel found. Water there was in plenty, but it did not come from a tap. It flowed from a spring outside, which rose up from the ground and went to a brook. Grey Rabbit cooked on a fire, but it was a wood fire, there was no coal in that part of the country. Tea did not come from India, but from a little herb known very well to country people, who once dried it and used it in their cottage homes. Bread was baked from wheat ears, ground fine, and Hare and Grey Rabbit gleaned in the cornfields to get the wheat.

The doormats were plaited rushes, like country-made mats, and cushions were stuffed with wool gathered from the hedges where sheep pushed through the thorns. As for the looking-glass, Grey Rabbit found the glass, dropped from a lady's handbag, and Mole made a frame for it. Usually the animals gazed at themselves in the still pools as so many country children have done. The country ways of Grey Rabbit were the country ways known to the author.

ONE DAY, when Grey Rabbit was walking in the lane, she saw a tiny spire of blue smoke twisting from the hedge. She walked very softly, on tiptoe, for who knows what it might be? Smoke means fire, and fire means a somebody.

She sniffed at the smell of smoke, and it was very sweet, like the burning of cherry-wood. Then another smell came to her. It was a savoury stew. She took a step, and listened, and then she took another step and cocked her ears, and waited. Somebody was busy; she could hear the rattle of sticks and the chink of a tin can.

THEN A VOICE began to sing, in
a high, thin, little squeak—
" I haven't got a coat, and I haven't
got a shoe,
I haven't got a penny, and I haven't
got a sou.
I don't care a jot, I've got my
cooking-pot,
And the whole wide world is mine to
wander through."
There sat a ragged little Hedgehog,
dark and dirty and dusty.

HIS EYES TWINKLED, and he stirred a round tin pan over the fire with a wooden spoon. He danced a step, and waved the spoon, and Grey Rabbit squatted behind the broad leaves of a dock. She thought he hadn't seen her, and she was very much surprised when he called out to her :

" Grey Rabbit, Grey Rabbit. I see you hiding there. Come out."

Shyly she stepped from her shelter and stood before him.

" Well, Grey Rabbit, you don't know me, do you? "

" No," faltered Grey Rabbit, " I've not seen you before."

" I am a wanderer. I travel the world. You stay at home in your little house at the end of the wood, but I go everywhere, up and down the country: England, Ireland, Scotland and Wales."

"YES, I have heard Milkman Hedgehog speak of you," said Grey Rabbit. "You must be Brush, the Wandering Hedgehog."

"True! I haven't a roof over my head, Grey Rabbit. In the winter, I sleep in a small hut in yonder oak tree across the pasture, but the rest of the year I enjoy myself, seeing life."

"You seem to be very happy, out here in the lane," said Grey Rabbit, looking at his ancient hat, with the blue feather from a jay stuck in the side.

"WILL YOU TASTE my good broth, Grey Rabbit?" asked the ragged Hedgehog. "It's excellent. Even you and your friends have never tasted anything better, I'll wager." He took the pot off the cherry-wood fire, and ladled out a few spoonfuls into a little wooden bowl. He held it out to her, then took another bowl, and filled it for himself.

"Sit here, Grey Rabbit." He patted a tuft of moss, and Grey Rabbit smoothed her blue apron and seated herself opposite to him. She sipped the good broth, and it was indeed delicious. It tasted of bracken and ferns, parasol mushrooms and umbrella toadstools— all the wild things of the hedges.

"GREY RABBIT," said the Hedgehog, as he drank noisily, "Grey Rabbit, will you do me a favour?"

"Yes?" She opened her eyes wide, and watched him.

"Did you hear my song? Well, it's true I haven't a coat, and I wondered if you have a cast-off, left-off, done-with, forgotten and thrown-away coat of Mister Hare's that I could have?"

"Oh, yes," said Grey Rabbit quickly.

"It's cold, wandering the world. It's cold in the winter, before I get to my little house in the oak tree. And I should be real obliged, Miss Grey Rabbit."

"OH, YES," said Grey Rabbit again. "There's a nice red coat of Hare's. It will be rather large, I fear, but I could alter it to fit you."

"Thank you, kind Grey Rabbit. In return, I would like to give you a present." He cut a piece of an elder stem and made a little whistle out of it. When Grey Rabbit put it to her lips and blew hard, a lovely mellow note came from it. The chaffinches cried, "Pink, Pink," and the blackbirds flew down, and the tomtits turned head over heels in the hedges, they liked the music so much.

SO GREY RABBIT sat by the fire
with the Wandering Hedgehog,
while he told her tales. Once she leaned
over and put a branch on the flames,
and she watched the sparks fly upward.
She blacked her face, and she tore her
apron on a briar bush, but she didn't
care. It was lovely sitting in the lane,
watching the ragged little Hedgehog.

At last she remembered the family at
home, and she said good-bye.

" I won't forget the coat, Mr. Brush,"
she called as she tripped away.

Hare was swinging on the garden
gate, looking for her. Squirrel was
sitting in the apple tree.

"THERE YOU ARE AT LAST, Grey Rabbit," said Hare crossly. "We are as hungry as hunters. Where have you been all this time?"

"Oh, Squirrel and Hare, I've been talking to Brush the Wandering Hedgehog," cried Grey Rabbit excitedly.

"That dirty old ragamuffin!" exclaimed Squirrel, turning up her little nose and sliding from the tree.

"That beggarly old Hedgehog!" cried Hare, and he banged the gate. "Really, Grey Rabbit, you ought to have more sense."

"Did he pick your pocket?" asked Squirrel.

"Did he beg anything from you?" asked Hare.

"HE WAS VERY NICE, and you mustn't call him a dirty old ragamuffin. He may be dirty, but what is dirt? It is only the good mother earth. He may be ragged, but rags are jolly. I like rags."

Grey Rabbit was indignant.

" And he didn't pick my pocket, and there was nothing in it if he had done. He gave me an elder whistle to play," she continued.

" Go on, Grey Rabbit," said Hare sternly, when the little Rabbit stopped for breath. " I can see by your eye that there is something else."

" Yes," said Grey Rabbit. " He hasn't a coat and he asked if we could give him one."

"A COAT?" cried Hare, and he dragged his own coat tightly about him.

"A coat?" said Squirrel, sniffing, and she shook her long tail.

"Whose coat?" asked Hare.

"Yes, whose?" echoed Squirrel. "Coats don't grow on hedges."

"Your coat, Hare," murmured Grey Rabbit.

"My coat!" Hare leapt so high in surprise that his head touched the apple tree and knocked off some of the blossom.

"GREY RABBIT, what did you say?"

"I told him he could have your coat."

The two animals were speechless. Then Hare took another leap and Grey Rabbit nearly fell down with fright.

"Over my dead body," said he.

"Nobody else has a coat," said Grey Rabbit, almost in tears. "Squirrel hasn't one and I have only a cloak. He could have that."

"He can't have your blue cloak, Grey Rabbit," said Squirrel quickly. "I wear it when it's cold. We all wear it. Even Fuzzypeg is wrapped up in it."

"I HAVE TWO COATS," said Hare importantly, "a blue one for weekdays and a red one for Sundays. I shan't give either to any old Wandering Hedgehog in the lane."

"I'm hungry," said Squirrel. "I suppose you had dinner with that Hedgehog?"

"Well, I did," confessed Grey Rabbit.

"You did? Oh, Grey Rabbit! You will become a raggle-taggle gipsy if you go on like this. Look at your apron. You've torn it. Look at your face. There's a black mark across it."

" I TORE my apron on the briar bush," whispered Grey Rabbit, sadly, " and I smudged my face helping Brush to stir his fire."

" Well! Well! Well! " They could say no more.

They all went indoors where the fire was low and the potatoes were roasting in the embers. Soon Grey Rabbit had a nice meal ready of hot potatoes in their jackets, with a nut of butter and a pinch of salt, and mugs of milk.

When she looked out of the window, she could see the thin blue spire of smoke coming from the hedge far away, and she thought of the Wandering Hedgehog sitting there all alone. She did want to give him a coat.

HARE RAN lollopy-lollopy over the field and peered through the bushes at the Hedgehog.

He sat on a tuffet of moss, smoking an old clay pipe, reading a newspaper made of last year's brown leaves. The news was quite a year old, but that didn't matter. Hare kept very still.

Brush put down his newspaper and began to sing :

" I haven't got a coat, and I haven't got
    a shoe,
  I haven't got a penny, and I haven't
    got a sou.
  I don't care a jot, I've got my cook-
    ing-pot,
  And the whole wide world is mine to
    wander through."

HARE NEVER MOVED, or blinked an eye.

" Thank you for the coat, Hare," called the Hedgehog. " It will suit me nicely. Thank you for your kind thought."

" Eh? " exclaimed the Hare, jumping with surprise. " You can't have my coat." He buttoned his jacket more closely around him.

" Well, anybody's coat will do," said the Hedgehog lazily.

Hare stared at him, and then came closer. He sniffed the sweet-smelling fire and he sniffed the Hedgehog's baccy.

"DRIED MEDDER-SWEET," remarked the Hedgehog. "You like a puff, Hare?"

"Well, I hardly think, I'm sure I don't know," stammered Hare.

"Come along. It won't bite you," said the Hedgehog, and held out the dirty old pipe in his black wrinkled hand. Hare wiped it on his handkerchief, and then he took a puff.

It was delicious! He took another puff. Really, it was glorious! He kept puffing, and the meadow-sweet smoke came out, and mingled with the smoke of the cherry-wood fire.

THEN HARE noticed something very strange. As the smoke curled upward it formed lovely shapes of trees and animals and hills. He could see in it old farm-houses, and children playing, and rabbits racing on the common, and lambs leaping and birds flying.

" See anything? " asked the Wandering Hedgehog.

" Yes. Lots of things! Yes," cried Hare excitedly.

" Them's my wanderings. They get into my baccy and comes out in smoke, and all I have to do to remember them is to sit back and smoke my pipe. Would you like a pipe for yourself, Hare? "

THE HEDGEHOG stretched up and cut a slip of elder wood. He hollowed it and made a pipe with an acorn cup for the bowl.

" Here you are," said he. " Smoke it when Grey Rabbit isn't looking." He winked and nodded, his roguish eye flashed, and Hare came closer.

The Wandering Hedgehog gave the fire a kick, and a blaze shot up. Then he put the kettle on, filled with water from the spring.

" Have a cup of tea, Mister Hare? " he asked.

" I DON'T MIND if I do," said the fascinated Hare.

He watched the dark little fellow's hands move swiftly and surely, putting a pinch of green tea in the kettle, bringing a can of milk from under some leaves, and producing two wooden bowls. Then the Hedgehog poured out the steaming tea, and they both sipped.

" Like it? " asked the Hedgehog.

" I should think I do. What's it made of? "

" Just tea—a few herbs and some secret things," said the Hedgehog.

" Put something on the fire, Hare."

Hare leaned forward and threw a log on the blaze.

"NOW ABOUT THIS COAT," went on the Hedgehog amiably. "I don't want to rob you, Hare, but if you can get me a coat for the hard weather, well, I shall say 'Thank ye.' If, howsomedever you can't, well, I shall say 'Thank ye,' just the same."

That seemed fair enough to Hare, and he went home to talk it over with Grey Rabbit and Squirrel.

"The Wandering Hedgehog isn't such a bad fellow," he began carelessly, as he sat down.

"Oh," said Squirrel quickly. "How do you know?"

"I just met him, when I was out. I just had a hobnob with him," said Hare.

" HARE! You've been smoking. I can smell baccy on your clothes." Squirrel wrinkled her little nose and sniffed.

" Well, yes," confessed Hare. " I had a pipe with him, and he gave me a little baccy pipe for myself."

" And you've got a smudge on your cheek," said Squirrel.

Hare rubbed his face with his coat sleeve and Grey Rabbit laughed aloud.

"DID YOU PUT A LOG on the fire, Hare?" she asked.

"Yes, I did," said Hare. "I say, Grey Rabbit and Squirrel, can we get a coat for that Hedgehog? He hasn't one, and when the frost comes he will feel cold."

"That dirty old ragamuffin!" cried Squirrel.

"He's not so dirty, Squirrel. I like a bit of dirt myself. It's mother earth, as Grey Rabbit says," said Hare, with a sly glance at the laughing Grey Rabbit.

Now, later on, Squirrel stepped daintily down the lane, swinging on the bushes, and running along the branches so that she wouldn't be seen.

SHE PEERED from an overhanging larch tree at the blue curl of smoke rising from the fire. The Wandering Hedgehog was frying something on a toasting-fork made from a twiggy branch. There was a good smell and a sizzle, and Squirrel leaned forward to look. She over-balanced and fell nearly on top of the Hedgehog.

" Good evening, Miss Squirrel," said he, helping her to tidy herself. " I seed you a-peeping at me. Welcome to my fireside."

Squirrel was a good deal ruffled by her fall, but the Hedgehog went back to his cooking. He kept his twinkling eyes on the toasting-fork.

" What are you doing? " asked Squirrel, overcome with curiosity.

"IT'S A PARASOL mushroom I'm toasting for supper," replied the Hedgehog. "Would you like a taste, Miss?"

Squirrel sniffed and sniffed, and found the smell delicious.

"Yes, please," said she demurely.

"Sit yourself on the tuffet," said the Hedgehog, and he patted a cushion of moss.

So Squirrel tucked her dress round her and sat down and watched the old ragamuffin. The fire flickered, and blue flames shot up. She leaned forward and warmed her paws and looked around her.

THE HEDGEHOG was black and dirty, but his face was pleasant and he had a merry smile. His little hat was perched sideways on his head. His narrow green waistcoat was buttoned with strange shining buttons.

" Will you have a bite of supper with me, Miss Squirrel? " he asked.

" Yes, please," said Squirrel. She felt hungry, although she had had a good tea.

The Hedgehog poured out a bowl of nettle broth, flavoured with wild marjoram and clover, and Squirrel sipped it with a wooden spoon. Then Hedgehog gave her a toasted mushroom, black and juicy.

IT WAS REALLY VERY TASTY and Squirrel nibbled the edges, and even licked her paws at the end.

Then the Hedgehog stretched out a skinny hand and pulled up a flowering rush. He peeled it, so that it was like an ivory wand. Then he twisted it into a bracelet and held it out to Squirrel. She slipped it on her arm and smiled graciously at him.

Hedgehog talked slowly of this and of that, speaking of his journeys and adventures.

" When I was in Africky, I had golden mushrooms that grew in the deserts. Nothing grew except those mushrooms. The sun toasted them for me. It was easy living there."

"OH, INDEED," said Squirrel, opening wide her eyes.

"When I was at the North Pole, I had snow mushrooms. They grew on the ice-fields. I just ate them, cooked in the beams of the moon, Miss Squirrel."

"Oh, indeed," said Squirrel, gasping with surprise.

"About this coat, Miss Squirrel. If you could see your way to getting a coat for me, I should be much obliged," said he.

"Certainly," said Squirrel. "But how did you manage without one at the North Pole?"

" **I** HAD ONE THERE," said the Hedgehog. " Made of Polar-bear skin it was, but it got lost at sea. I was wrecked and lost everything I had."

" Poor Wandering Hedgehog," murmured Squirrel. " Yes, I will see if I can persuade Hare and Grey Rabbit to find you a coat."

She went off home and told her tale.

" So you've been to see the Wandering Hedgehog," teased Hare. " He's such a dirty old ragamuffin, I wonder you went."

" You've got a smudge on your face, Squirrel. Did you put a log on the fire? " asked Grey Rabbit.

"REALLY WE MUST get a coat for that poor animal," said Squirrel indignantly. "There you two sit, and nobody bothers to get a coat for a poor, lonely old beggar."

"So at last we are all agreed," laughed Grey Rabbit.

She went to the chest of drawers and hunted among the few clothes there. She brought out some pieces of cloth, green and blue and red.

"Those wouldn't make a coat for a bumble-bee," said Hare. "I'll go and ask everyone for some scraps, Grey Rabbit. I'm sure our friends have some bits and bobs stored away."

THE NEXT DAY when Milkman Hedgehog came to the door with the breakfast milk, Hare asked him.

" There's a poor relation of yours down the lane with never a coat to his back," said he severely. " What are you going to do about it? "

" Him? That Wandering Hedgehog? " Old Hedgehog scratched his head and pondered.

" He can wrap a piece of sacking round him when it rains, same as I do. What does he want with a coat? I've got no coat, neither has our Fuzzypeg."

" You have smocks," said Hare sternly.

"WELL, he should wear a smock, but he won't. However, if you go and talk it over with my Missis, she'll maybe find you a bit of something."

Hare visited Mrs. Hedgehog, and explained what he wanted.

"I'll give you a red spotted handkerchief," said she. "It will help. And here's a bit of an old blue smock of Fuzzypeg's."

Hare next went to see Moldy Warp the Mole, in his house in the field.

"That Wandering Hedgehog?" cried Moldy Warp, shaking his head.

"I know him. He's a romancer, he is. I'll give him a piece of black velvet, if that's any use."

THEN HARE went to Water-rat's house. Water-rat was rowing in his little boat when Hare hailed him.

"Something to make a coat for the Wandering Hedgehog?" asked Water-rat. "Something for that old vagabond? Here's a boat cushion, made of strong red cloth." He tossed a cushion ashore and Hare caught it.

"Thank you, Water-rat. This will suit the Hedgehog. Thank you, old fellow," called Hare, and away he ran home with it.

Then he went to see Wise Owl in the wood. Wise Owl muttered and grumbled when Hare rang his bell.

"Be off! Be off! I'm sleepy," he cried, and he threw a book at Hare. He banged his door and got back to bed.

HARE PICKED UP the book, and hurried back to Grey Rabbit with it.

" We can't sew this," said he. " He can't be dressed in paper. What is it called, Grey Rabbit? "

Grey Rabbit examined it, and turned the coloured pages.

" The ' Cutter and Tailor. How to make a coat out of bits and pieces,' " she read. " This is splendid. This will be a great help. It's got a picture of a patchwork coat."

So Hare went to all the other houses to find some more pieces. He brought home such a collection of scraps and oddments, of silk and wool, of leaves and lichens, of calico and linen, that Grey Rabbit threw up her paws when she saw them all.

"IT'S LUCKY we've Wise Owl's book to tell us how to make it," said she. They sat round the table with all the scraps spread out and planned the coat. Grey Rabbit stitched them together as Squirrel and Hare sorted them into shapes and colours. It was a fine patchwork, with golden yellow, and brown and orange, with blue and scarlet and crimson and black velvet.

Grey Rabbit used all the coloured cottons in her work basket, and Squirrel embroidered the edges of the coat with feather-stitching and an embroidery stitch of her own called " Squirrel-knots."

"IT'S MOST BEAUTIFUL," she cried, when at last Grey Rabbit held it up for all to see.

" It's like the rainbow," said Hare.

" It's like a garden full of flowers," said Squirrel poetically.

" Let's take it to him now," cried Hare, leaping up.

Out they went in the moonlight, dancing with joy down the lane, tossing the little coat, and laughing with happiness. There was the little fire burning with the sweet scent of cherry-wood, and by its side sat Brush, the Wandering Hedgehog. Although they walked very softly when they were near, I think he heard them, for he spoke and stirred his fire so that sparks flew out.

"HALLO, SQUIRREL, and Hare and Little Grey Rabbit. Have you brought it?"

"Yes, Brush. It's nicer than my old red coat," said Hare. "You are lucky this time."

"A coat of twenty colours," added Squirrel. "At least Fuzzypeg says there are twenty. I can't count so many."

"Ah, my nephew, Fuzzypeg. He's a Scholar," said the Wandering Hedge-hog proudly.

THEY HELD up the coat in the firelight and the dirty old Hedgehog took his pipe from his mouth and stared.

"Never, never did I see a coat like this, not in all my born days," said he. "Nay, I'm wrong.

"Only once did I see one, and that was worn by the Emperor of China. Yes, when I was in China, the Emperor had a coat, but not as good as this."

He slipped his arms through the sleeves and buttoned the acorns down the front. He held up the sides and danced a clumsy dance, while the three friends looked on.

"Thank you all for your kindness to a poor fellow. Old Wandering Hedgehog won't forget you."

HE DIVED INTO the hedgerow and pulled out a little brown basket.

"Here's something for you in exchange. Don't open it till you get home," said he. "I shall be off on my travels to-night. I was just waiting for this coat, which I knowed was coming, and the new moon, and I knowed that was coming too, and the evening star. Now I shall be off."

"Where are you going, Brush? I wish you were staying here," said Grey Rabbit.

"THANK YOU for that kind thought, Grey Rabbit. I'm going far, to Canada, across the ocean in a steamer. So good-bye, my dear friends."

" Good-bye and good luck," they answered. The Wandering Hedgehog was already stamping out the fire. He gathered up his bundle and cooking-pots and stick. Then away he turned down the lane, with his little hat perched jauntily on his head and his pipe in his mouth.

THEY STARED after him. They could hear his voice in the distance, singing his old song, with a slight difference :

" I've got a fine coat, and I haven't got
  a shoe,
  I haven't got a penny, and I haven't
  got a sou.
  I don't care a jot, I've got my
  cooking-pot,
  And the whole wide world is mine to
  wander through."

"WHAT'S IN THE BASKET?"
asked Hare, trying to peep
through. the lid.

"Wait till we get home," warned
Grey Rabbit.

So away they ran, leaping under the
thin new moon, back to their house.
They stood around while Hare took the
wooden pin from the basket and lifted
the lid.   Inside lay a little brown
Nightingale. She sang a sweet trilling
song and then she flew out.

" SHE MAY MAKE HER NEST in our garden," said Grey Rabbit. " Will you, dear Nightingale? "

The Nightingale sang again, as if to agree that it was just the place she wanted.

So she built her nest with the help of her little brown husband in the apple tree, and there she sat on her eggs. Every night Mr. Nightingale sang, and every day as well. It was better even than having a musical box, Grey Rabbit thought.

Far away the Wandering Hedgehog roamed the lanes. He carried his coloured coat in his pack, to keep it clean, ready for the cold weather. He had a long way to go, but, whether he went to Canada, I cannot say, for he was always a romancer.

THE END OF THE STORY